Beckett's Guide to Baby Mama Drama for Dummies

SE Hall

Cover designed by Dana Leah

Formatted by Brenda Wright – Formatting Done Wright

All these late nights...she doesn't care WHAT you say, only HOW you say it...so me and my P been writing a book. She's my proof-listener.

I'm thinking "Beckett's Guide to Baby Mama Drama For Dummies (this means YOU dude)" is the perfect title.

No, I don't care if you have a MBA and all the guys at your country club think your paisley socks are classy and real men wear pink...your fancy ass don't know everything, so listen up!

DISCLAIMER (Dane said I had to put this in or somebody might get butt hurt and sue me.)

This manual is one man's attempt to help all you other clueless schmucks out there survive your Shorty, aka wife, girlfriend, baby mama, woman who's about to make your life hell as you never knew it, being pregnant. None of this information has been researched, vouched for clinically and/or Googled. I did not survey several different pregnant women, at different stages in term, from all walks of life, nor were there any pie charts and/or focus groups involved. Information contained herein is as unscientific at it gets, but I'm a smart fucking guy, so when your buddy reads it and walks by you all smiley while you're rocking back and forth in the corner, crying, contemplating suicide... don't say I didn't warn ya.

Now that Dane's happy, all asses covered, here we go.

For the official step by step, I'm gonna start you at the beginning. I have tried to keep each point short and sweet, the "manbonics' version, easier for you to understand. If you want the long, every scenario possible, weepy eyed drawn out version- go ask your woman, or your pansy ass bros who have kids and are so fucking happy you stopped by for a beer and they have another man to talk to, they'll ramble on in narratives the likes of which would have me cracking their teeth.

This here is done Sawyer style.

If you see me out and want to thank me, and you will want to thank me, buy me a beer and we're even. OR...well no, not or, just do this...keep your son the hell away from my daughter, FOREVER.

Chapter One

Your New Psalms

The minute she says "I'm pregnant!" run like shit is chasing you, to buy the "other" book. The *What to Expect* one. As infinite as my wisdom is, this one's better. Consider it your Bible. Wrap it in plastic so it doesn't get wet. Put a Clapper on it so you never lose it. Pet it, fondle it, become one with it. Highlight anything you didn't know and earmark as many pages as you need to. Sleep with it, your arm wrapped around it, 'cause A. Soon your woman won't want you touching her anyway, and B. If you're touching the book, your chances of the powers of osmosis helping out your male-and-therefore-not-equipped-for-the-realm-you-have-just-entered-brain-even-as-you-sleep greaten. Trust me, you need all the extra help you can get. To go with your new book, buy a dictionary or make buds with Siri and tell her to have that shit on tap at all times! You will not know at least 20% of the words, let alone their gravity, in this book. No, looking at the pictures, no matter how many times you turn the book sideways and upside down, won't help you get it either. Consult the dictionary. And when you still don't quite understand, see below.

Buy a thesaurus... find a word you DO know what it means, go back and apply it in the original sentence.

The single most crucial fact to know about this book? Do NOT just go throwing your knowledge in your woman's face. Practice how you're going to say it, and the facial expression to accompany, *several* times in the mirror before *actually* speaking.

Examples:

CORRECT: "You're exactly right, Angel." Insert smile. "And I'm thrilled I studied up on this so I can best help you, because this is about you and only you. In fact, have I said yet today that you're beautiful and I love you?" Blow her a kiss.

INCORRECT: "That's not what the book said."

Even if you'd bet your balls that the book said differently, **you're mistaken**. Even when you consult it and read again, removing all doubt that she was wrong, **you're mistaken**. Nope, **you're mistaken**.

Unless it's something absolutely dangerous, like say lighting up a cigar while changing a cat litter box, let. It. Go.

For those of you dumbfuck know-it-alls who must simply not place value on her EVER PUTTING OUT AGAIN, still shaking your head, all "I don't read unless it's a magazine while I pinch off a loaf..." May the force be with you and your chafed right hand.

Chapter Two

No Grabbin' the Funbags

If you don't know what funbags are, I'm surprised you were man enough to knock her up in the first place. I won't even make you shamefully go find the book/dictionary/thesaurus for this. They're her tits, dumbass!

One of the earliest symptoms of pregnancy is tender boobs. So if your lady is one who indulges your love of breasts, lets you fondle them, squeeze 'em, and suck on 'em 'til your heart's content and dick is buried...find your inner gentle or new playground, because those beauts are closed for your kind of business. You risk putting her completely out of the mood, even crying in pain and kicking you out of the bed and room, if you even so much as graze the side of one too hard.

My advice is to stay below the navel and perfect a new talent. But if she grabs your hand and places it back on her breast, stay calm and let her lead.

This is one of the hardest steps to master, because not only are your hands always itching to play with them—I feel your pain, brother—but they get bigger! Out of nowhere, one day, they've doubled in size, thus doubling your temptation and urge to latch onto one for dear life. No can do. Turn and walk away, then go roll your balls around in your hand and do the best you can to picture her ever-inflating mounds of pleasure in your head as you do so. And yes, this is the best plan I've got.

I myself am a tit man and was pained to the core when I got grounded, so I definitely put a lot of thought into alternatives. There are none, at least not any that won't get you killed; a.k.a. do not go grabbing strangers' racks, crying out desperately that you just miss it!

And if you do break, and subsequently get arrested, do NOT call your woman to bail you out. Call your buddy who your woman hates, that she'd never talk to. Always think ahead at least two steps down the "what's the worst that could happen" road. That's the path you need to stay on 'til you're straight in the head again.

Chapter Three

The Walking Sprinkler

This one should be pretty self-explanatory, but I'll spell it out for you because I know, I know...you're so confused and terrified these days, your balls are all shrunk up and inverted, and NOTHING is self-explanatory anymore.

Your pregnant angel is going to piss a lot more than a lot. In fact, you'll begin to notice she's outputting more than she drinks. She'll pee more out in one day than she drank in all of last week, by the hour, every hour. Doesn't matter if you're watching the game, or eating a nice dinner, or have friends over, or you're already in bed. She needs to tinkle.

She needed to tinkle before you sat down or got settled or walked out the door, she just didn't say anything.

***NOWHERE in this book am I able to explain the ONE vow of silence she takes. Quit looking. At least half the time, you're going to have to stop whatever it is you were doing and join her, or walk her there, or hold her stuff while she goes—basically making you an intricate part of the tenth through eighty-fifth pee production of that, and every other, day.

That's about it on this topic, but a couple handy side notes I experienced firsthand that I thought important, and fucking hilarious, enough to mention.

1. Do NOT, under any circumstances, tickle her. This is no longer a flirtatious, covert form of foreplay. It's begging for her to piss on you, plain and simple.

2. Do NOT take a shower with her unless she "went" right before she hopped in with you. The sound of running water calls to her and she WILL piss directly on your foot, smiling innocently and trying to distract you so that you don't notice the sudden warmer pool you're standing in.

3. Long road trips—cancel them. Or don't even bother setting the cruise control. You'll be start/stop the entire time.

Chapter Four

Nausea, Crying, and Crying to the Point of Nausea

I'm trying to K.I.S.S. it for you men out there (Keep It Simple, Stupid) and have combined these two "issues" into one chapter because honestly, they start pretty much at the same time—DAY ONE—and stop pretty much at the same time—NO TELLING—it's different for each woman.

Let's start with the throwing up. It's going to happen sporadically, anytime, anywhere and you, my friend, must become immune to the sight and smell; gagging yourself only urges her to puke more. You must also develop super powers, able to pull a car across three lanes of traffic to the shoulder at the first gagging noise lest you begin paying repeatedly for car detailing or are some deranged fucker who chooses to clean it yourself. And if you forget to have barf bags stashed in every vehicle, room, and in your pocket on every trip you make outside of your home—well, you asked for it.

Restaurants, friends' houses, stores...pretty much anywhere you're not sure of what smell will linger inside at any given time are your danger zones. And even then, a smell she loved on Tuesday might detonate the pyrotechnics on Thursday, so basically, Boy Scout that shit. ALWAYS BE PREPARED, because it's a crap shoot.

The most important piece of advice on this is: AVOID KISSING HER ON THE MOUTH. Because...well, her breath smells like vomit more often than not. Kisses on the cheek, end of her nose, and forehead seemed to appease my girl, so stick with these plus a lovey dovey look when you do it. Get it wrong and you're either in for a bout of hurt feelings of epic, hormonal proportions...or sucking face with puke breath.

And the crying; again, anytime, anywhere over anything. Danger zones on these are: chick flicks and commercials, especially ones for fabric softener, ASPCA, and/or greeting cards. During holiday seasons, when mushy commercials are rampant, break something in your TV that only you can "fix" while she's asleep in order to catch up on ESPN.

You will also need to build up your tolerance for getting easily embarrassed. Practice giving your audience the whole subtle "she's pregnant" universal mouthing and smile where everyone goes "ahhh, been there," and goes about their business.

Neither of these things are the worst of it, so master these first and easily; you'll need your strength and honing skills reserved for what's to come!

Chapter 5

Her Sex Drive: Floor it til' the Wheels Fall Off

Now every woman is different (so I've read), but between my own Baby Mama and the three movies she's made me watch, I'm calling bullshit on any article that gives you even the slightest hope their drive is heightened during the whole pregnancy.

My money and best advice is staying on a merciful, dick-saving window of bliss at approximately 14-16 weeks. Any earlier than that, her time is most likely spent slowly trudging in the direction leading to food, anywhere she sees fit to sleep, a place to throw up, or a soak in a hot tub. But one glorious day around 15 weeks, she wakes up feeling great, with this sudden, almost frightening burst of energy and an exaggerated, anything-but-frightening state of horny.

Like, first met, anywhere you could get away with it horny.

Take it. Any position, any time, any place. Call in to work. Turn off your phone. Tell anyone you know you moved. Because again, in my experience, this too shall pass in the blink of an eye and you don't want to waste a second of it.

And I've seen no actual proof the Secret Cavern of Vagina opens again until around 8-10 weeks *after* the baby is born.

A couple *key* tips for this wrinkle in time:

1.   Get in there. Gently, but IN THERE. You absolutely, 100%, *cannot* poke or stab the baby in the head with your dick. No, not even you, "Long Dong." *You wish*. I asked—every doctor, nurse, reception desk lady, and hotline I could find. I even sent a picture of what I'm packing to one nurse, certain she didn't understand the actual threat I imposed. She didn't appreciate it, judging by the written request we change OBGYN Clinics, yet she was kind enough to reaffirm that it's not possible.

So do it like a crazed man digging for gold. Gently.

2. If you don't like Doggie Style (which you're a moron if not), LEARN TO. It's the most comfortable for her. In fact, she might actually moan instead of complain and quit in the middle of it...and it's deep penetration. You're a man, a "dog" by nature—own it. Her on top is good too, especially since her tits are getting bigger and jiggle like shiny, hypnotic gems, but she will most likely hold back a little and/or get a cramp, so encourage the DAWG.

3. If she's not in the mood or changes her mind mid-nirvana, don't even bother begging for a "finish me off BJ." Not only will she hiss about your insensitivity, but her gag reflex is on overdrive and she'll be making excruciating noises—not the good kind—seconds away from puking on your dick, before she's even made it past the head.

4. Bottom line—capitalize on any come hither eyes or invitations with Doggie Style, then go buy lotion in bulk.

I wish I had better news for you, and God Bless those of you whose women are "Miss Defy the Odds." Just don't go bragging as you're likely to get throat punched by a backed-up Dad to Be because nobody likes a fucking showoff. But for those of us in the majority—lotion and solidarity, my brothers.

Chapter 6

Cravings

No, not that kind, read back a chapter, dumbass.

Weird, horrendously timed *food* cravings are your next hurdle. You've probably always heard the time-old "pickles and ice cream" story. It would be nice if it was that simple.

They *may* ask for that, but it won't be every single time. And even if and when they do, it's not just pickles and ice cream. It's a certain brand, size, and flavor of pickles and a certain brand and flavor of ice cream. And the minute you set the bag down in front of her, beaming like the Superman Shopper you feel, it's changed to imported sushi only sold at that one market on the other side of town and a slice of spiced fruitcake—*in August*—while you were gone.

The good news is she'll change her mind again any second and not only will she no longer be teetering between breaking down in sobs or throwing the bag at your head, but you won't really have to go find fruitcake in August.

The smart thing to do is Plan B your Plan B. Which translates to stock up on the things she asks for most and be ready to whip them out at all times, dangling the delicacy in front of her face 'til she caves and all but rips your hand off to grab it.

Also, you should have already done this yesterday—buy a deep freezer. Then stock that mother to the brim with these "sure bet" treats we've just discussed. Serious as shit, when you go to the store—you know, at least every other day—buy every. Single. One. They. Have.

One what, you ask? Yep, that. And that. Those too.

Most importantly, sleep fully dressed, because the above won't always work, and off you go at three am. Deal with it, you are now the new "Time to Make the Donuts" dude wandering aimlessly through town half asleep. At least with this tip, you won't be doing so in your underwear.

When you have nailed the entrée of the hour, DO NOT rest the plate or bowl on her belly. She only finds this endearing about 10% of the time. And God forbid your baby choose that moment to kick and spill it...apocalypse now.

And *never*, I repeat *never*, take the last bite or throw the remains away. It is *without fail* the very first thing she will look for when the next wave of ravenous hunger ensues.

Your best bet is to always eat out and for the love of your balls being attached to your body, throw all evidence of such traitorous activity away in a roadside dumpster. Then air out your car—I'm talking swing every door open and shut like you want your vehicle to fly away—because she'll smell the french fries the minute you turn onto your street.

Gum and breath mints are good to keep handy at all times too, on the off chance she actually wants to kiss you.

Don't be scared. Be smart. Be prepared.

Chapter 7

You're Almost on Your Own, Bro

Seven is my number, so I'm going to combine two pearls of wisdom into this last chapter then wish you the best of luck. You can do it! Men have come out the other side alive for centuries, there's hope for you too.

Scales

No.

That's pretty much it, NO.

Search your house right now, load them all in your car and hurl them into the deepest body of water nearest you.

If she buys a new one, "accidentally" break it.

When they weigh her at doctor visits, you have two options. Institute whichever you feel most comfortable with and can pull off covertly.

1. Slip the nurse a twenty spot to lie by ten pounds

2. Solemnly swear to your beautiful woman that you were so engrossed in sharing these "small moments" with her that you got distracted and accidentally leaned against the scale.

Another heads up: the freaks of nature ladies in Lamaze that look like they haven't gained a pound WILL get mentioned, most likely after every damn class. When your woman is bawling, having already flown over the cuckoo's nest and circled back around to you, and asking what you think, there are only two acceptable responses.

A. "Who? Gorgeous, I have no clue who you're talking about. All those trolls blend into one big glob, really."

B. "Her? Well thank God she didn't gain too much more weight than you, which she *so* did, because her hook nose and the huge booger in it are unfortunate enough, my beauty."

Practice in a mirror, you *will* get put on this spot and have to be convincing.

Mood Swings

Not a damn thing you can do about this little perk. I got absolutely nothing.

Some of them are actually kind of cute, others are fleeting, and the rest...all men have selective hearing, right? Activate that survival trait when needed.

In Closing

One day soon, you'll have the woman you love back, plus fuller breasts, luscious, prominent curves, and a certain look she gives your child that makes *you* feel a mood swing coming on.

Your baby will wrap their tiny hand around your finger and coo as they sleep on your chest...and you'll be ready to impregnate your lady all over again. Trust me.

Good luck and congratulations! Just the fact you actually read the book, even if it was on the toilet, shows you'll willing to do what it takes to survive.

It's absolutely worth the ride.

You're Welcome,

Sawyer Beckett, Proud Father of Princess P

"Spread the diaper in the position of the diamond with you at bat. Then fold second base down to home and set the baby on the pitcher's mound. Put first base and third together, bring up home plate and pin the three together. Of course, in case of rain, you gotta call the game and start all over again."

-Jimmy Piersal, 1968

As written in a card by Laney Jo Walker. Go figure.

Click here to read the next book in the Evolve series….

*Endure

Reading Order for the Evolve Series

*Emerge
*Embrace
Entangled
*Entice
Sawyer Beckett's Baby Mama Drama Guide For Dummies
*Endure
Sawyer Beckett's Guide for Tools Looking to Date My Daughter
Entwined
*Embody
A Crew Christmas
Elusive (Princess Presley Duet Book One)
Exclusive (Princess Presley Duet Book Two)

Books by S.E. Hall

(all books can be found on Amazon; those with a * indicate additional availability in audio format)

~Standalone~

*Unstable
books2read.com/u/mdN9dd

~Finally Found Novels~

*Pretty Instinct
books2read.com/u/4jw7Xk

*Pretty Remedy:
books2read.com/u/mgr6pX

~Evolve Series~

*Emerge
books2read.com/u/bOaqyo

*Embrace
books2read.com/u/m0x9lM

*Entangled
books2read.com/u/mvjVW2

(Evolve Series 2.5)

*Entice
books2read.com/u/ml5kAW

Sawyer Beckett's Baby Mama Drama Guide For Dummies
books2read.com/u/478qQg

(An Evolve Series Companion Novella)

*Endure
books2read.com/u/3J0qpX

Sawyer Beckett's Guide for Tools Looking to Date My Daughter
books2read.com/u/4jwOP5

(An Evolve Series Companion Novella)

Entwined
books2read.com/u/boYk8a

(An Evolve Series Wedding Novella)

A Crew Christmas
books2read.com/u/3Ro76x

(An Evolve Series Holiday Special)

~Full Circle Series~

The Evolve Spinoff Series

*Embody
books2read.com/u/bxqkQe

Elusive
books2read.com/u/47ZBzR

Exclusive
books2read.com/u/4jD7eY

(Princess Presley Duet Book Two)

˜Smokin' Hot Shorts˜

Full Body Check
http://books2read.com/u/31OMZ6

Laid Over
http://books2read.com/u/mvKV0l

Yes, Officers
Co-written with Hilary Storm

Quarterback Sack
books2read.com/u/3nOk25

Pick Your Pleasure
http://books2read.com/u/bzPyWq

(The Hearts Desire Series)

Co-written with Angela Graham

*Stirred Up
books2read.com/u/mgrejR

*Packaged
books2read.com/u/bPJdyz

*Handled
books2read.com/u/4EDvlg

*Lights, Camera...Reality

books2read.com/u/m2o1Y7

(Matched)

One Naughty Night
books2read.com/u/4DoqKk

(Harmony/Evolve crossover Novella)

Filthy Foreign Exchange
books2read.com/u/bpWkwk

Filthy Foreign Exchange 2
Co-written with Ashley Suzanne

Accidentally On Purpose
books2read.com/u/3L9qy5

Co-written with Erin Noelle

Conspire
books2read.com/u/4Awlpd

S.E. Hall

putting the *S.E.* in *sex*

S.E. Hall is the New York Times & USA Today bestselling author of the Evolve Series, the Full Circle Series/a spinoff of the Evolve Series, standalone contemporary romances Pretty Instinct, Pretty Remedy and Unstable, and her Smokin' Hot Shorts- Laid Over and Full Body Check, published in multiple countries and languages.

Hall has also co-written with authors Angela Graham, Erin Noelle, Hilary Storm and Ashley Suzanne.

S.E. Hall resides in Arkansas with her husband of 23 years, and together, they have four amazing daughters, ages 28, 23, 17 and 16, and three beautiful grandchildren.

Stay connected with S.E. Hall:

BookBub: https://www.bookbub.com/authors/s-e-hall
Facebook: https://www.facebook.com/S.E.HallAuthorEmerge
Twitter: https://twitter.com/Sehallauthor
Amazon: http://www.amazon.com/S.E.-Hall/e/B00D0AB9TI/
Goodreads:
https://www.goodreads.com/author/show/7087549.S_E_Hall
Instagram: https://instagram.com/Sehall_author/

Professional Inquiries
S.E. Hall is represented by SBR Media; any questions/interest regarding Hall's work(s) can be directed to Stephanie Phillips via email at stephanie@sbrmedia.com

Made in the USA
Monee, IL
29 May 2021